'I LIKE
HUN
SHE ___
AT ME.'

C000130091

ANAÏS NIN
Born 1903, Neuilly-sur-Seine, France
Died 1977, Los Angeles, USA

In the early 1940s, Anaïs Nin began writing erotica at a dollar a page for an unnamed 'collector'. These pieces were later published in the 1970s. 'The Veiled Woman', 'Linda' and 'Marianne' first appeared in the collection *Delta of Venus* (1977), and 'Mandra' in *Little Birds* (1979).

NIN IN PENGUIN MODERN CLASSICS
A Spy in the House of Love
Delta of Venus
Henry and June
Little Birds

ANAÏS NIN

The Veiled Woman

PENGUIN BOOKS

PENGUIN CLASSICS

UK | USA | Canada | Ireland | Australia
India | New Zealand | South Africa

Penguin Books is part of the Penguin Random House group
of companies whose addresses can be found at
global.penguinrandomhouse.com.

This selection first published 2018
007

Copyright © the Anaïs Nin Trust, 1977, 1979

The moral rights of the author have been asserted

All rights reserved

Set in 10.25/12.75 pt Dante MT Std
Typeset by Jouve (UK), Milton Keynes
Printed and bound in Great Britain by Clays Ltd, Elcograf S.p.A.

ISBN: 978-0-241-33954-1

www.greenpenguin.co.uk

Penguin Random House is committed to a
sustainable future for our business, our readers
and our planet. This book is made from Forest
Stewardship Council® certified paper.

Contents

The Veiled Woman

George once went to a Swedish bar he liked, and sat at a table to enjoy a leisurely evening. At the next table he noticed a very stylish and handsome couple, the man suave and neatly dressed, the woman all in black, with a veil over her glowing face and brilliant colored jewelry. They both smiled at him. They said nothing to one another, as if they were very old acquaintances and had no need to talk.

The three of them watched the activity at the bar – couples drinking together, a woman drinking alone, a man in search of adventures – and all seemed to be thinking the same things.

Finally the neatly dressed man began a conversation with George, who now had a chance to observe the woman at length and found her even more beautiful. But just when he expected her to join in the conversation, she said a few words to her companion that George could not catch, smiled, and glided off. George was crestfallen. His pleasure in the evening was gone. Furthermore, he had only a few dollars to spend, and he could not invite the man to drink with him and discover perhaps a little more about the woman. To his surprise, it was the man who turned to him and said, 'Would you care to have a drink with me?'

George accepted. Their conversation went from experiences with hotels in the South of France to George's admission that he was badly in need of money. The man's response implied that it was extremely easy to obtain money. He did not go on to say how. He made George confess a little more.

Now George had a weakness in common with many men; when he was in an expansive mood, he loved to recount his exploits. He did this in intriguing language. He hinted that as soon as he set foot in the street some adventure presented itself, that he was never at a loss for an interesting evening, or for an interesting woman.

His companion smiled and listened.

When George had finished talking, the man said, 'That is what I expected of you the moment I saw you. You are the fellow I am looking for. I am confronted with an immensely delicate problem. Something absolutely unique. I don't know if you have had many dealings with difficult, neurotic women – No? I can see that from your stories. Well, I have. Perhaps I attract them. Just now I am in the most intricate situation. I hardly know how to get out of it. I need your help. You say you need money. Well, I can suggest a rather pleasant way of making some. Listen carefully. There is a woman who is wealthy and absolutely beautiful – in fact, flawless. She could be devotedly loved by anyone she pleased, she could be married to anyone she pleased. But for one perverse accident of her nature – she only likes the unknown.'

'But everybody likes the unknown,' said George, thinking

immediately of voyages, unexpected encounters, novel situations.

'No, not in the way she does. She is interested only in a man she has never before and never will see again. And for this man she will do anything.'

George was burning to ask if the woman was the one who had been sitting at the table with them. But he did not dare. The man seemed to be rather unhappy to have to tell, and yet was impelled to tell, this story. He continued, 'I have this woman's happiness to watch over. I would do anything for her. I have devoted my life to satisfying her caprices.'

'I understand,' said George. 'I could feel the same way about her.'

'Now,' said the elegant stranger, 'if you would like to come with me, you could perhaps solve your financial difficulties for a week, and incidentally, perhaps, your desire for adventure.'

George flushed with pleasure. They left the bar together. The man hailed a taxi. In the taxi he gave George fifty dollars. Then he said he was obliged to blindfold him, that George must not see the house he was going to, nor the street, as he was never to repeat this experience.

George was in a turmoil of curiosity now, with visions of the woman he had seen at the bar haunting him, seeing each moment her glowing mouth and burning eyes behind the veil. What he had particularly liked was her hair. He liked thick hair that weighed a face down, a gracious burden, odorous and rich. It was one of his passions.

The ride was not very long. He submitted amiably to all

the mystery. The blindfold was taken off his eyes before he came out of the taxi so as not to attract the attention of the taxi driver or doorman, but the stranger had counted wisely on the glare of the entrance lights to blind George completely. He could see nothing but brilliant lights and mirrors.

He was ushered into one of the most sumptuous interiors he had ever seen – all white and mirrored, with exotic plants, exquisite furniture covered in damask and such a soft rug that their footsteps were not heard. He was led through one room after another, each in different shades, all mirrored, so that he lost all sense of perspective. Finally, they came to the last. He gasped slightly.

He was in a bedroom with a canopied bed set on a dais. There were furs on the floor and vaporous white curtains at the windows, and mirrors, more mirrors. He was glad that he could bear these repetitions of himself, infinite reproductions of a handsome man, to whom the mystery of the situation had given a glow of expectation and alertness he had never known. What could this mean? He did not have time to ask himself.

The woman who had been at the bar entered the room, and just as she entered, the man who had brought him to the place vanished.

She had changed her dress. She wore a striking satin gown that left her shoulders bare and was held in place by a ruffle. George had the feeling that the dress would fall from her at one gesture, strip from her like a glistening sheath, and that underneath would appear her glistening skin, which shone like satin and was equally smooth to the fingers.

He had to hold himself in check. He could not yet believe that this beautiful woman was offering herself to him, a complete stranger.

He felt shy, too. What did she expect of him? What was her quest? Did she have an unfulfilled desire?

He had only one night to give all his lover's gifts. He was never to see her again. Could it be he might find the secret to her nature and possess her more than once? He wondered how many men had come to this room.

She was extraordinarily lovely, with something of both satin and velvet in her. Her eyes were dark and moist, her mouth glowed, her skin reflected the light. Her body was perfectly balanced. She had the incisive lines of a slender woman together with a provocative ripeness.

Her waist was very slim, which gave her breasts an even greater prominence. Her back was like a dancer's, and every undulation set off the richness of her hips. She smiled at him. Her mouth was soft and full and half-open. George approached her and laid his mouth on her bare shoulders. Nothing could be softer than her skin. What a temptation to push the fragile dress from her shoulders and expose the breasts which distended the satin. What a temptation to undress her immediately.

But George felt that this woman could not be treated so summarily, that she required subtlety and adroitness. Never had he given to his every gesture so much thought and artistry. He seemed determined to make a long siege of it, and as she gave no sign of hurry, he lingered over her bare shoulders, inhaling the faint and marvelous odor that came from her body.

He could have taken her then and there, so potent was the charm she cast, but first he wanted her to make a sign, he wanted her to be stirred, not soft and pliant like wax under his fingers.

She seemed amazingly cool, obedient but without feeling. Never a ripple on her skin, and though her mouth was parted for kissing, it was not responsive.

They stood there near the bed, without speaking. He passed his hands along the satin curves of her body, as if to become familiar with it. She was unmoved. He slipped slowly to his knees as he kissed and caressed her body. His fingers felt that under the dress she was naked. He led her to the edge of the bed and she sat down. He took off her slippers. He held her feet in his hands.

She smiled at him, gently and invitingly. He kissed her feet, and his hands ran under the folds of the long dress, feeling the smooth legs up to the thighs.

She abandoned her feet to his hands, held them pressed against his chest now, while his hands ran up and down her legs under the dress. If her skin was so soft along the legs, what would it be then near her sex, there where it was always the softest? Her thighs were pressed together so he could not continue to explore. He stood and leaned over her to kiss her into a reclining position. As she lay back, her legs opened slightly.

He moved his hands all over her body, as if to kindle each

little part of it with his touch, stroking her again from shoulders to feet, before he tried to slide his hand between her legs, more open now, so that he could almost reach her sex.

With his kisses her hair had become disheveled, and the dress had fallen off her shoulders and partly uncovered her breasts. He pushed it off altogether with his mouth, revealing the breasts he had expected, tempting, taut, and of the finest skin, with roseate tips like those of a young girl.

Her yielding almost made him want to hurt her, so as to rouse her in some way. The caresses roused him but not her. Her sex was cool and soft to his finger, obedient, but without vibrations.

George began to think that the mystery of the woman lay in her not being able to be aroused. But it was not possible. Her body promised such sensuality. The skin was so sensitive, the mouth so full. It was impossible that she should not feel. Now he caressed her continuously, dreamfully, as if he were in no hurry, waiting for the flame to be kindled in her.

There were mirrors all around them, repeating the image of the woman lying there, her dress fallen off her breasts, her beautiful naked feet hanging over the bed, her legs slightly parted under the dress.

He must tear the dress off completely, lie in bed with her, feel her whole body against his. He began to pull the dress down, and she helped him. Her body emerged like that of Venus coming out of the sea. He lifted her so that she would lie fully on the bed, and his mouth never ceased kissing every part of her body.

Then a strange thing happened. When he leaned over to feast his eyes on the beauty of her sex, its rosiness, she quivered, and George almost cried out for joy.

She murmured, 'Take your clothes off.'

He undressed. Naked, he knew his power. He was more at ease naked than clothed because he had been an athlete, a swimmer, a walker, a mountain climber. And he knew then that he could please her.

She looked at him.

Was she pleased? When he bent over her, was she more responsive? He could not tell. By now he desired her so much that he could not wait to touch her with the tip of his sex, but she stopped him. She wanted to kiss and fondle it. She set about this with so much eagerness that he found himself with her full backside near his face and able to kiss and fondle her to his content.

By now he was taken with the desire to explore and touch every nook of her body. He parted the opening of her sex with his two fingers, he feasted his eyes on the glowing skin, the delicate flow of honey, the hair curling around his fingers. His mouth grew more and more avid, as if it had become a sex organ in itself, capable of so enjoying her that if he continued to fondle her flesh with his tongue he would reach some absolutely unknown pleasure. As he bit into her flesh with such a delicious sensation, he felt again in her a quiver of pleasure. Now he forced her away from his sex, for fear she might experience all her pleasure merely kissing him and that he would be cheated of feeling himself inside of her womb. It was as if they both had become ravenously hungry for the taste of flesh. And now their two mouths melted into each other, seeking the leaping tongues.

Her blood was fired now. By his slowness he seemed to have done this, at last. Her eyes shone brilliantly, her mouth could not leave his body. And finally he took her, as she offered herself, opening her vulva with her lovely fingers, as if she could no longer wait. Even then they suspended their pleasure, and she felt him quietly, enclosed.

Then she pointed to the mirror and said, laughing, 'Look, it appears as if we were not making love, as if I were merely sitting on your knees, and you, you rascal, you have had it inside me all the time, and you're even quivering. Ah, I can't bear it any longer, this pretending I have nothing inside. It's burning me up. Move now, move!'

She threw herself over him so that she could gyrate around his erect penis, deriving from this erotic dance a pleasure which made her cry out. And at the same time a lightning flash of ecstasy tore through George's body.

Despite the intensity of their lovemaking, when he left, she did not ask him his name, she did not ask him to return. She gave him a light kiss on his almost painful lips and sent him away. For months the memory of this night haunted him and he could not repeat the experience with any woman.

One day he encountered a friend who had just been paid lavishly for some articles and invited him to have a drink. He told George the spectacular story of a scene he had witnessed.

He was spending money freely in a bar when a very distinguished man approached him and suggested a pleasant pastime, observing a magnificent love scene, and as George's friend happened to be a confirmed voyeur, the suggestion met with instant acceptance. He had been taken to a mysterious house, into a sumptuous apartment, and concealed in a dark room, where he had seen a nymphomaniac making love with an especially gifted and potent man.

George's heart stood still. 'Describe her,' he said.

His friend described the woman George had made love to, even to the satin dress. He also described the canopied bed, the mirrors, everything. George's friend had paid one hundred dollars for the spectacle, but it had been worthwhile and had lasted for hours.

Poor George. For months he was wary of women. He could not believe such perfidy, and such play-acting. He became obsessed with the idea that the women who invited him to their apartments were all hiding some spectator behind a curtain.

Linda

Linda stood in front of her mirror examining herself critically in full daylight. Now past thirty, she was becoming concerned with her age, although nothing about her betrayed any lessening of her beauty. She was slender, youthful in appearance. She could well deceive everyone but herself. In her own eyes her flesh was losing some of its firmness, some of that marble smoothness that she had admired so often in her own mirror.

She was no less loved. If anything she was more loved than ever, because now she attracted all the young men who sense that it is from such a woman that they will really learn the secrets of lovemaking, and who feel no attraction to the young girls of their age who are backward, innocent, inexperienced, and still possessed by their families.

Linda's husband, a handsome man of forty, had loved her with the fervor of a lover for many years. He closed his eyes to her young admirers. He believed that she did not take them seriously, that her interest was due to her childlessness and the need to pour her protective feelings over people who were beginning to live. He himself was reputed to be a seducer of women of all classes and character.

She remembered that on her wedding night André had been an adoring lover, worshiping each part of her body separately, as if she were a work of art, touching her and marveling, commenting on her ears, her feet, her neck, her hair, her nose, her cheeks, and her thighs, as he fondled them. His words and voice, his touch, opened her flesh like a flower to the heat and light.

He trained her to be a sexually perfect instrument, to vibrate to every form of caress. One time he taught her to put the rest of her body to sleep, as it were, and to concentrate all her erotic feelings in her mouth. Then she was like a woman half-drugged, lying there, her body quiet and languid, and her mouth, her lips, became another sex organ.

André had a particular passion for her mouth. In the street he looked at women's mouths. To him the mouth was indicative of the sex. A tightness of a lip, thinness, augured nothing rich or voluptuous. A full mouth promised an open, generous sex. A moist mouth tantalized him. A mouth that opened out, a mouth that was parted as if ready for a kiss, he would follow doggedly in the street until he could possess the woman and prove again his conviction of the revelatory powers of the mouth.

Linda's mouth had seduced him from the first. It had a perverse, half-dolorous expression. There was something about the way she moved it, a passionate unfolding of the lips, promising a person who would lash around the beloved like a storm. When he first saw Linda, he was taken into her through this mouth, as if he were already making love to her. And so it was on their wedding night. He was obsessed with her mouth. It was on her mouth that he threw himself, kissing it until it burned, until the tongue was worn out, until the lips were swollen; and then, when he had fully aroused her mouth, it was thus that he took her, crouching over her, his strong lips pressed against her breasts.

He never treated her as a wife. He wooed her over and over again, with presents, flowers, new pleasures. He took her to dinner at the *cabinets particuliers* of Paris, to the big restaurants, where all the waiters thought she was his mistress.

He chose the most exciting food and wine for her. He made her drunk with his caressing words. He made love to her mouth. He made her say that she wanted him. Then he would ask: 'And how do you want me? What part of you wants me tonight?'

Sometimes she answered, 'My mouth wants you, I want to feel you in my mouth, way down in my mouth.' Other times she answered, 'I am moist between the legs.'

This is how they talked across restaurant tables, in the small private dining rooms created especially for lovers. How discreet the waiters, knowing when not to return. Music would come from an invisible source. There would be a divan. When the meal was served, and André had pressed Linda's knees between his and stolen kisses, he would take her on the divan, with her clothes on, like lovers who do not have time to undress.

He would escort her to the opera and to the theaters famed for their dark boxes, and make love to her while they watched a spectacle. He would make love to her in taxis, in a barge anchored in front of Notre Dame that rented cabins to lovers. Everywhere but at home, on the marital bed. He would drive her to little far-off villages and stay at romantic inns with her. He would take a room for them in the luxurious houses of prostitution he had known. Then he would treat her like a prostitute. He would make her submit to his whims, ask to be whipped, ask her to crawl on her hands and knees and not to kiss him but to pass her tongue all over him like an animal.

These practices had aroused her sensuality to such a degree that she was frightened. She was afraid of the day when André would cease to be sufficient for her. Her sensuality was, she knew, vigorous; his was the last burst of a man who had spent himself on a life of excess and now gave her the flower of it.

A day came when André had to leave her for ten days for a trip. Linda was restless and feverish. A friend telephoned her, André's friend, the painter of the day in Paris, the favorite of all women. He said to her, 'Are you bored with yourself, Linda? Would you care to join us in a very special kind of party? Do you have a mask?'

Linda knew exactly what he meant. She and André had often laughed at Jacques's parties in the Bois. It was his favorite form of amusement: on a summer night, to gather society people wearing masks, drive to the Bois with bottles of champagne, find a clearing in the wooded section and disport themselves.

She was tempted. She had never participated in one. That, André had not wanted to do. He said playfully that the question of the masks might confuse him and that he did not want to make love to the wrong woman.

Linda accepted the invitation. She put on one of her new evening dresses, a heavy satin dress which outlined her body like a wet glove. She wore no underwear, no jewelry that could identify her. She changed her hair style, from a page-boy frame around her face to a pompadour style, which revealed the shape of her face and neck. Then she tied the black mask on her face, pinning the elastic to her hair for greater security.

At the last minute she decided to change the color of her hair and had it washed and tinted blue-black instead of pale blonde. Then she put it up again and found herself so altered that it startled her.

About eighty people had been asked to meet at the big studio of the fashionable painter. It was dimly lit so as to preserve the guests' identities better. When they were all there, they were whisked to the waiting automobiles. The chauffeurs knew where to go. In the deepest part of the woods there was a beautiful clearing covered with moss. There they sat, having sent the chauffeurs away, and began to drink champagne. Many of the caresses had already begun in the crowded automobiles. The masks gave people a liberty that turned the most refined ones into hungry animals. Hands ran under the sumptuous evening dress to touch what they wanted to touch, knees intertwined, breaths came quicker.

Linda was pursued by two men. The first of them did all he could to arouse her by kissing her mouth and breasts, while the other, with more success, caressed her legs under her long dress, until she revealed by a shudder that she was aroused. Then he wanted to carry her off into the darkness.

The first man protested but was too drunk to compete. She was carried away from the group to where the trees made dark shadows and lowered onto the moss. From nearby there were cries of resistance, there were grunts, there was a woman shrieking, 'Do it, do it, I can't wait any more, do it, do it to me!'

The orgy was in full bloom. Women caressed one another. Two men would set about teasing a woman into a frenzy and then stop merely to enjoy the sight of her, with her dress half-undone, a shoulder strap fallen, a breast uncovered, while she tried to satisfy herself by pressing obscenely against the men, rubbing against them, begging, lifting her dress.

Linda was astonished by the bestiality of her aggressor. She, who had known only the voluptuous caresses of her husband, found herself now in the grip of something infinitely more powerful, a desire so violent it seemed devouring.

His hands gripped her like claws, he lifted her sex to meet his penis as if he did not care if he broke her bones in doing so. He used *coups de beliér*, truly like a horn entering her, a goring that did not hurt but which made her want to retaliate with the same fury. After he had satisfied himself once with a wildness and violence that stunned her, he whispered, 'Now I want you to satisfy yourself, fully, do you hear me? As you never did before.' He held his erect penis like a primitive wooden symbol, held it out for her to use as she wished.

He incited her to unleash her most violent appetite on him. She was hardly aware of biting into his flesh. He panted in her ears, 'Go on, go on, I know you women, you never really let yourself take a man as you want to.'

From some depths of her body that she had never known, there came a savage fever that would not spend itself, that could not have enough of his mouth, his tongue, his penis inside of her, a fever that was not content with an orgasm. She felt his teeth buried in her shoulder, as her teeth bit into his neck, and then she fell backward and lost consciousness.

When she awakened, she was lying on an iron bed in a shabby room. A man was asleep beside her. She was naked, and he too, but half-covered by the sheet. She recognized the body which had crushed her the night before in the Bois. It was the body of an athlete, big, brown, muscular. The head was handsome, strong, with wild hair. As she looked at him admiringly, he opened his eyes and smiled.

'I could not let you go back with the others, I might never have seen you again,' he said.

'How did you get me here?'

'I stole you.'

'Where are we?'

'In a very poor hotel, where I live.'

'Then you're not . . .'

'I'm not a friend of the others, if that is what you mean. I am simply a workman. One night, bicycling back from my work, I saw one of your *partouzes*. I got undressed and joined it. The women seemed to enjoy me. I was not discovered. When I had made love to them, I stole away. Last night I was passing by again and I heard the voices. I found you being kissed by that man, and I carried you off. Now I have brought you here. It may make trouble for you, but I could not give you up. You're a real woman, the others are feeble compared to you. You've got fire.'

'I have to leave,' said Linda.

'But I want your promise that you will come back.'

He sat up and looked at her. His physical beauty gave him a grandeur, and she vibrated at his nearness. He began to kiss her and she felt languid again. She put her hand on his hard penis. The joys of the night before were still running through her body. She let him take her again almost as if to make sure that she had not dreamed. No, this man who could make his penis burn through her whole body and kiss her as if it were to be the last kiss, this man was real.

And so Linda returned to him. It was the place where she felt most alive. But after a year she lost him. He fell in love with another woman and married her. Linda had become so accustomed to him that now everyone else seemed too delicate, too refined, too pale, feeble. Among the men she knew, there was none with that savage strength and fervor of her lost lover. She searched for him again and again, in small bars, in the lost places of Paris. She met prizefighters, circus stars, athletes. With each she tried to find the same embraces. But they failed to arouse her.

When Linda lost the workman because he wanted to have a woman of his own, a woman to come home to, a woman who would take care of him, she confided in her hairdresser. The Parisian hairdresser plays a vital role in the life of a

Frenchwoman. He not only dresses her hair, about which she is particularly fastidious, but he is an arbiter of fashion. He is her best critic and confessor in matters of love. The two hours that it takes to get one's hair washed, curled and dried is ample time for confidences. The seclusion of the little cabinet protects secrets.

When Linda had first arrived in Paris from the little town in the South of France where she was born and she and her husband had met, she was only twenty years old. She was badly dressed, shy, innocent. She had luxuriant hair which she did not know how to arrange. She used no make-up. Walking down the Rue Saint-Honoré admiring the shop windows, she became fully aware of her deficiencies. She became aware of what the famous Parisian chic meant, that fastidiousness of detail which made of any woman a work of art. Its purpose was to heighten her physical attributes. It was created largely by the skill of the dressmakers. What no other country was ever able to imitate was the erotic quality of French clothes, the art of letting the body express all its charms through clothes.

In France they know the erotic value of heavy black satin, giving the shimmering quality of a wet naked body. They know how to delineate the contours of the breast, how to make the folds of the dress follow the movements of the body. They know the mystery of veils, of lace over the skin, of provocative underwear, of a dress daringly slit.

The contour of a shoe, the sleekness of a glove, these give the Parisian woman a trimness, an audacity, that far surpasses the seductiveness of other women. Centuries of coquetry have produced a kind of perfection that is apparent not only in the rich women but in the little shop girls. And the hairdresser is the priest of this cult for perfection. He tutors the women who come from the provinces. He refines vulgar women; he brightens pale women; he gives them all new personalities.

Linda was fortunate enough to fall into the hands of Michel, whose salon was near the Champs Elysées. Michel was a man of forty, slender, elegant and rather feminine. He spoke suavely, had beautiful salon manners, kissed her hand like an aristocrat, kept his little mustache pointed and glazed. His talk was bright and alive. He was a philosopher and a creator of women. When Linda came in, he cocked his head like a painter who is about to begin a work of art.

After a few months Linda emerged a polished product. Michel became, besides, her confessor and director. He had not always been a hairdresser of well-to-do women. He did not mind telling that he had begun in a very poor quarter where his father was a hairdresser. There the women's hair was spoiled by hunger, by cheap soaps, carelessness, rough handling.

'Dry as a wig,' he said. 'Too much cheap perfume. There was one young girl – I have never forgotten her. She worked for a dressmaker. She had a passion for perfume but could not afford any. I used to keep the last of the toilet-water bottles for her. Whenever I gave a woman a perfume rinse, I saw to it that a little was left in the bottle. And when Gisele came I liked to pour it down between her breasts. She was so delighted that she did not notice how I enjoyed it. I would take the collar of her dress between my thumb and forefinger, pull it out a little, and drop the perfume down, stealing a glance at her young breasts. She had a voluptuous way of moving afterward, of closing her eyes and taking in the smell and reveling in it. She would cry out sometimes, "Oh, Michel, you've wet me too much this time." And she would rub her dress against her breasts to dry herself.

'Then once I could not resist her any more. I dropped the perfume down her neck, and when she threw her head back and closed her eyes, my hand slipped right to her breasts. Well, Gisele never came back.

'But that was only the beginning of my career as a perfumer of women. I began to take the task seriously. I kept perfume in an atomizer and enjoyed spraying it on the breasts of my clients. They never refused that. Then I learned to give them a little brushing after they were ready. That's a very enjoyable task, dusting the coat of a well-formed woman.

'And some women's hair puts me in a state which I cannot describe to you. It might offend you. But there are women whose hair smells so intimate, like musk, that it makes a man – well, I cannot always keep myself under control. You know how helpless women are when they are lying back to have their hair washed, or when they are under the dryer, or having a permanent.'

Michel would look a client over and say, 'You could easily get fifteen thousand francs a month,' which meant an apartment on the Champs Elysées, a car, fine clothes, and a friend who would be generous. Or she might become a woman of the first category, the mistress of a senator or of the writer or actor of the day.

When he helped a woman reach the position due her, he maintained her secret. He never talked about anybody's life except in disguised terms. He knew a woman married for ten years to the president of a big American corporation. She still had her prostitute's card and was well known to the police and to the hospitals where the prostitutes went for weekly examinations. Even today, she could not become altogether accustomed to her new position and at times forgot that she had the money in her pocket to tip the men who waited on her during her Clipper trip across the ocean. Instead of a tip she handed out a little card with her address.

It was Michel who counseled Linda never to be jealous, that she must remember there were more women in the world than men, especially in France, and that a woman must be generous with her husband – think how many women would be left without a knowledge of love. He said this seriously. He thought of jealousy as a sort of miserliness. The only truly generous women were the prostitutes, actresses, who did not withhold their bodies. To his mind, the meanest type of woman was the American gold digger who knew how to extract money from men without giving herself, which Michel thought a sign of bad character.

He thought that every woman should at one time or another be a whore. He thought that all women, deep down, wished to be a whore once in their lives and that it was good for them. It was the best way to retain a sense of being a female.

When Linda lost her workman, therefore, it was natural for her to consult Michel. He advised her to take up prostitution. That way, he said, she would have the satisfaction of proving to herself that she was desirable entirely apart from the question of love, and she might find a man who would treat her with the necessary violence. In her own world she was too worshiped, adored, spoiled, to know her true value as a female, to be treated with the brutality that she liked.

Linda realized that this would be the best way to discover whether she was aging, losing her potency and charms. So she took the address Michel gave her, got into a taxi and was taken to a place on the Avenue du Bois, a private house with a grandiose appearance of seclusion and aristocracy. There she was received without questions.

'*De bonne famille?*' That was all they wanted to ascertain. This was a house which specialized in women *de bonne famille*. Immediately the caretaker would telephone a client: 'We have a newcomer, a woman of most exquisite refinement.'

Linda was shown into a spacious boudoir with ivory furniture, brocade draperies. She had taken off her hat and veil and was standing before the large gold-framed mirror arranging her hair, when the door opened.

The man who came in was almost grotesque in appearance. He was short and stout, with a head too big for his body, features like an overgrown child's, too soft and hazy and tender for his age and bulk. He walked very swiftly toward her and kissed her hand ceremoniously. He said, 'My dear, how wonderful it is that you were able to escape from your home and husband.'

Linda was about to protest when she became aware of the man's desire to pretend. Immediately she fell into the role but trembled within herself at the thought of yielding to this man. Already her eyes were turning towards the door, and she wondered if she could make her escape. He caught her glance and said very quickly, 'You need not be afraid. What I ask of you is nothing to be frightened about. I am grateful to you for risking your reputation to meet me here, for leaving your husband for me. I ask very little, this presence of yours here makes me very happy. I have never seen a woman more beautiful than you are, and more aristocratic. I love your perfume, and your dress, your taste in jewelry. Do let me see your feet. What beautiful shoes. How elegant they are, and what a delicate ankle you have. Ah, it is not very often that so beautiful a woman comes to see me. I have not been lucky with women.'

Now it seemed to her that he looked more and more like a child, everything about him, the awkwardness of his gestures, the softness of his hands. When he lit a cigarette and smoked, she felt that this must be his first cigarette, because of the awkward way he handled it and the curiosity with which he watched the smoke.

'I cannot stay very long,' she said, impelled by the need to escape. This was not at all what she had expected.

'I will not keep you very long. Will you let me see your handkerchief?'

She offered him a delicate, perfumed handkerchief. He smelled it with an air of extreme pleasure.

Then he said, 'I have no intention of taking you as you expect me to. I am not interested in possessing you as other men do. All I ask of you is that you pass this handkerchief between your legs and then give it to me, that is all.'

She realized that this would be so much easier than what she had feared. She did it willingly. He watched her as she leaned over, raised her skirt, unfastened the lace pants and passed the handkerchief slowly between her legs. He leaned over then and put his hand over the handkerchief merely to increase the pressure and so that she would pass it again.

He was trembling from head to foot. His eyes were dilated. Linda realized that he was in a state of great excitement. When he took the handkerchief away he looked at it as if it were a woman, a precious jewel.

He was too absorbed to talk. He walked over to the bed, laid the handkerchief on the bedspread and then threw himself on it, unbuttoning his trousers as he fell. He pushed and rubbed. After a moment he sat up on the bed, wrapped his penis with the handkerchief and then continued jerking, finally reaching an orgasm which made him cry out with joy. He had completely forgotten Linda. He was in a state of ecstasy. The handkerchief was wet from his ejaculation. He lay back panting.

Linda left him. As she walked through the hallways of the house she met the woman who had received her. The woman was amazed that she should want to leave so soon. 'I gave you one of our most refined clients,' she said, 'a harmless creature.'

It was after this episode that Linda sat in the Bois one day watching the parade of spring costumes on a Sunday morning. She was drinking in the colors and elegance and perfumes when she became conscious of a particular perfume near her. She turned her head. To her right sat a handsome man of about forty, elegantly dressed, with his glossy black hair carefully combed back. Was it from his hair that this perfume came? It reminded Linda of her voyage to Fez, of the great beauty of the Arab men there. It had a potent effect on her. She looked at the man. He turned and smiled at her, a brilliant white smile of big strong teeth with two smaller milk teeth, slightly crooked, which gave him a roguish air.

Linda said, 'You use a perfume which I smelled in Fez.'

'That's right,' said the man, 'I was in Fez. I bought this at the market there. I have a passion for perfumes. But since I found this one I have never used any other.'

'It smells like some precious wood,' said Linda. 'Men should smell like precious wood. I have always dreamed of finally reaching a country in South America where there are whole forests of precious woods which exude marvelous odors. Once I was in love with patchouli, a very ancient perfume. People no longer use it. It came from India. The Indian shawls of our grandmothers were always saturated with patchouli. I like to walk along the docks, too, and smell spices in the warehouses. Do you do that?'

'I do. I follow women sometimes, just because of their perfume, their smell.'

'I wanted to stay in Fez and marry an Arab.'

'Why didn't you?'

'Because I fell in love with an Arab once. I visited him several times. He was the handsomest man I had ever seen. He had a dark skin and enormous jet eyes, an expression of such emotion and fervor that it swept me off my feet. He had a thundering voice and the softest manner. Whenever he talked to anyone, he would stand, even in the street, holding their two hands, tenderly, as if he wanted to touch all human beings with the same great softness and tenderness. I was completely seduced, but . . .'

'What happened?'

'One day, when it was extremely hot, we sat drinking mint tea in his garden and he took off his turban. His head was completely shaved. It is the tradition of the Arabs. It seems that all their heads are completely shaved. That somehow cured me of my infatuation.'

The stranger laughed.

With perfect synchronization, they got up and started to walk together. Linda was as much affected by the perfume, which came from the man's hair, as she would have been by a glass of wine. Her legs felt unsteady, her head foggy.

Her breasts swelled and fell with the deep breaths she took. The stranger watched the heaving of her breasts as if he were watching the sea unfolding at his feet.

At the edge of the Bois he stopped. 'I live right up there,' he said, pointing with his cane to an apartment with many balconies. 'Would you care to come in and have an apéritif with me on my terrace?'

Linda accepted. It seemed to her that, were she deprived of the perfume which enchanted her, she would suffocate.

They sat on his terrace, quietly drinking. Linda leaned back languidly. The stranger continued to watch her breasts. Then he closed his eyes. Neither of them made a movement. Both had fallen into a dream.

He was the first to move. As he kissed her Linda was carried back to Fez, to the garden of the tall Arab. She remembered her sensations of that day, the desire to be enfolded in the white cape of the Arab, the desire for his potent voice and his burning eyes. The smile of the stranger was brilliant, like the smile of the Arab. The stranger *was* the Arab, the Arab with thick black hair, perfumed like the city of Fez. Two men were making love to her. She kept her eyes closed. The Arab was undressing her. The Arab was touching her with fiery hands. Waves of perfume dilated her body, opened it, prepared her to yield. Her nerves were set for a climax, tense, responsive.

She half opened her eyes and saw the dazzling teeth about to bite into her flesh. And then his sex touched her and entered her. It was like something electrically charged, each thrust sending currents throughout her body.

28

He parted her legs as if he wanted to break them apart. His hair fell on her face. Smelling it, she felt the orgasm coming and called out to him to increase his thrusts so that they could come together. At the moment of the orgasm he cried out in a tiger's roar, a tremendous sound of joy, ecstasy and furious enjoyment such as she had never heard. It was as she had imagined the Arab would cry, like some jungle animal, satisfied with his prey, who roars with pleasure. She opened her eyes. Her face was covered with his black hair. She took it into her mouth.

Their bodies were completely tangled. Her panties had been so hurriedly pulled down that they had fallen the length of her legs and lay around her ankles, and he had somehow inserted his foot into one half of the panties. They looked at their legs bound together by this bit of black chiffon, and they laughed.

She returned many times to this apartment. Her desire would begin long before each meeting, as she dressed for him. At all hours of the day his perfume would issue from some mysterious source and haunt her. Sometimes as she was about to cross a street, she would remember his scent so vividly that the turmoil between her legs would make her stand there, helpless, dilated. Something of it clung to her body and disturbed her at night when she was sleeping alone. She had never been so easily aroused. She had always needed time and caresses, but for the Arab, as she called him to herself, it seemed as if she were always erotically prepared, so much so that she was aroused long before he touched her, and what she feared was that she would come at the very first touch of his finger on her sex.

That happened once. She arrived at his apartment moist and trembling. The lips of her sex were as stiff as if they had been caressed, her nipples hard, her whole body quivering, and as he kissed her he felt her turmoil and slipped his hand directly to her sex. The sensation was so acute that she came.

And then one day, about two months after their liaison, she went to him and when he took her in his arms she felt no desire. He did not seem to be the same man. As he stood in front of her she coldly observed his elegance and his ordinariness. He looked like any elegant Frenchman one could see walking down the Champs Elysées, or at opening nights, or at the races.

But what had changed him in her eyes? Why did she not feel this great intoxication she felt ordinarily in his presence? There was something so usual now about him. So like any other man. So unlike the Arab. His smile seemed less brilliant, his voice less colorful. Suddenly she fell into his arms and tried to smell his hair. She cried out, 'Your perfume, you have no perfume on!'

'It's finished,' said the Arab Frenchman. 'And I cannot get any like it. But why should that upset you so?'

Linda tried to recapture the mood he threw her into. She felt her body grow cold. She pretended. She closed her eyes and she began to imagine. She was in Fez again, sitting in a garden. The Arab was sitting at her side, on a low, soft couch.

He had thrown her back on the couch and kissed her while the little water fountain sang in her ears, and the familiar perfume burned in an incense holder at her side. But, no. The fantasy was broken. There was no incense. The place smelled like a French apartment. The man at her side was a stranger. He was deprived of his magic that made her desire him. She never went to see him again.

Although Linda had not relished the adventure of the handkerchief, after a few months of not moving from her own sphere she became restless again.

She was haunted by memories, by stories she heard, by the feeling that everywhere around her men and women were enjoying sensual pleasure. She feared that now that she had ceased to enjoy her husband, her body was dying.

She remembered being sexually awakened by an accident at a very early age. Her mother had bought her panties that were too small for her and very tight between the legs. They had irritated her skin, and at night while falling asleep she had scratched herself. As she fell asleep, the scratching became softer and then she became aware that it was a pleasurable sensation. She continued to caress her skin and found that as her fingers came nearer the little place in the center, the pleasure increased. Under her fingers she felt a part which seemed to harden at her touch, and there found an even greater sensibility.

A few days later she was sent to confession. The priest sat at his chair and she was made to kneel at his feet. He was a Dominican and wore a long cord with a tassel which fell at his right side. As Linda leaned against his knees, she felt this tassel against her. The priest had a big warm voice which enveloped her, and he leaned down to talk to her. When she had finished with the ordinary sins – anger, lies and so on – she paused. Observing her hesitation, he began to whisper in a much lower tone, 'Do you ever have impure dreams?'

'What dreams, Father?' she asked.

The hard tassel that she felt just at the sensitive place between her legs affected her like her fingers' caresses of the nights before. She tried to move closer to it. She wanted to hear the voice of the priest, warm and suggestive, asking about the impure dreams. He said, 'Do you ever have dreams of being kissed, or of kissing someone?'

'No, Father.'

Now she felt that the tassel was infinitely more affecting than her fingers because, in some mysterious way or other, it was part of the priest's warm voice and his words, like 'kisses'. She pressed against him harder and looked at him.

He felt that she had something to confess, and asked, 'Do you ever caress yourself?'

'Caress myself how?'

The priest was about to dismiss the question, thinking his intuition had been an error, but the expression of her face confirmed his doubts.

'Do you ever touch yourself with your hands?'

It was at this moment that Linda wanted so much to be able to make one movement of friction and once again reach that extreme, overwhelming pleasure she had discovered a few nights ago. But she was afraid the priest would become aware and repulse her and she would lose the sensation completely. She was determined to hold his attention, and began, 'Father, it is true, I have something very terrible to confess. I scratched myself one night and then I caressed myself, and –'

'My child, my child,' said the priest, 'you must stop this immediately. It is impure. It will ruin your life.'

'Why is it impure?' asked Linda, pressing against the tassel. Her excitement was rising. The priest leaned over so close that his lips almost touched her forehead. She was dizzy. He said, 'Those are the caresses that only your husband can give you. If you do it and abuse them, you will grow weak, and no one will love you. How often have you done it?'

'For three nights, Father. I have had dreams too.'

'What sort of dreams?'

'I have had dreams of someone touching me there.'

Every word she said increased her excitement, and with a pretense of guilt and shame she threw herself against the priest's knees and bowed her head as if she would cry, but it was because the touch of the tassel had brought on the orgasm and she was shaking. The priest, thinking it was guilt and shame, took her in his arms, raised her from her kneeling position and comforted her.

Mandra

The illumined skyscrapers shine like Christmas trees. I have been invited to stay with rich friends at the Plaza. The luxury lulls me, but I lie in a soft bed sick with ennui, like a flower in a hothouse. My feet rest on soft carpets. New York gives me a fever – the great Babylonian city.

I see Lillian. I no longer love her. There are those who dance and those who twist themselves into knots. I like those who flow and dance. I will see Mary again. Perhaps this time I will not be timid. I remember when she came to Saint-Tropez one day and we met casually at a café. She invited me to come to her room in the evening.

My lover, Marcel, had to go home that night; he lived quite far away. I was free. I left him at eleven o'clock and went to see Mary. I was wearing my flounced Spanish cretonne dress and a flower in my hair, and I was all bronzed by the sun and feeling beautiful.

When I arrived, Mary was lying on her bed, cold-creaming her face, her legs and her shoulders, because she had been lying on the beach. She was rubbing cream into her neck, her throat – she was covered with cream.

This disappointed me. I sat at the foot of her bed and we

talked. I lost my desire to kiss her. She was running away from her husband. She had married him only to be protected. She had never really loved men but women. At the beginning of her marriage, she had told him all sorts of stories about herself that she should not have told him – how she had been a dancer on Broadway and slept with men when she was short of money; how she even went to a whorehouse and earned money there; how she met a man who fell in love with her and kept her for a few years. Her husband never recovered from these stories. They awakened his jealousy and doubts, and their life together had become intolerable.

The day after we met, she left Saint-Tropez, and I was filled with regrets for not having kissed her. Now I was about to see her again.

In New York I unfolded my wings of vanity and coquetry. Mary is as lovely as ever and seems much moved by me. She is all curves, softness. Her eyes are wide and liquid; her cheeks, luminous. Her mouth is full; her hair blonde, and luxuriant. She is slow, passive, lethargic. We go to the movies together. In the dark she takes my hand.

She is being analyzed and has discovered what I sensed long ago: that she has never known a real orgasm, at thirty-four, after a sexual life that only an expert accountant could keep track of. I am discovering her pretenses. She is always smiling, gay, but underneath she feels unreal, remote, detached from experience. She acts as if she were asleep. She is trying to awaken by falling into bed with anyone who invites her.

Mary says, 'It is very hard to talk about sex, I am so ashamed.'

She is not ashamed of doing anything at all, but she cannot talk about it. She can talk to me. We sit for hours in perfumed places where there is music. She likes places where actors go.

There is a current of attraction between us, purely physical. We are always on the verge of getting into bed together. But she is never free in the evenings. She will not let me meet her husband. She is afraid I will seduce him.

She fascinates me because sensuality pours from her. At eight years old she was already having a lesbian affair with an older cousin.

We both share the love of finery, perfume and luxury. She is so lazy, languid – purely a plant, really. I have never seen a woman more yielding. She says that she always expects to find the man who will arouse her. She has to live in a sexual atmosphere even when she feels nothing. It is her climate. Her favorite statement is, 'At that time, I was sleeping around with everybody.'

If we speak of Paris and of people we knew there, she always says, 'I don't know him. I didn't sleep with him.' Or, 'Oh yes, he was wonderful in bed.'

I have never once heard of her resisting – this, coupled with frigidity! She deceives everybody, including herself. She looks so wet and open that men think she is continuously in a state of near orgasm. But it is not true. The actress in her appears cheerful and calm, and inside she is going to pieces. She drinks and can sleep only by taking drugs. She always comes to me eating candy, like a schoolgirl. She looks about twenty. Her coat is open, her hat is in her hand. Her hair is loose.

One day she falls on my bed and knocks off her shoes. She looks at her legs and says, 'They are too thick. They are like Renoir legs, I was told once in Paris.'

'But I love them,' I say, 'I love them.'

'Do you like my new stockings?' She raises her skirt to show me.

She asks for a whiskey. Then she decides that she will take a bath. She borrows my kimono. I know that she is trying to tempt me. She comes out of the bathroom still humid, leaving the kimono open. Her legs are always held a little apart. She looks so much as if she were about to have an orgasm that one cannot help feeling: only one little caress will drive her wild. As she sits on the edge of my bed to put on her stockings, I cannot withhold any longer. I kneel in front of her and put my hand on the hair between her legs. I stroke it gently, gently, and I say, 'The little silver fox, the little silver fox. So soft and beautiful. Oh, Mary I can't believe that you do not feel anything there, inside.'

She seems on the verge of feeling, the way her flesh looks, open like a flower, the way her legs are spread. Her mouth is so wet, so inviting, the lips of her sex must be the same. She parts her legs and lets me look at it. I touch it gently and spread the lips to see if they are moist. She feels it when I touch her clitoris, but I want her to feel the bigger orgasm.

I kiss her clitoris, still wet from the bath; her pubic hair, still damp as seaweed. Her sex tastes like a seashell, a wonderful, fresh, salty seashell. Oh Mary! My fingers work more quickly, she falls back on the bed, offering her whole sex to me, open and moist, like a camellia, like rose petals, like velvet, satin. It is rosy and new, as if no one had ever touched it. It is like the sex of a young girl.

Her legs hang over the side of the bed. Her sex is open; I can bite into it, kiss it, insert my tongue. She does not move. The little clitoris stiffens like a nipple. My head between her two legs is caught in the most delicious vise of silky, salty flesh.

My hands travel upwards to her heavy breasts, caress them. She begins to moan a little. Now her hands travel downwards and join mine in caressing her own sex. She likes to be touched at the mouth of her sex, below the clitoris. She touches the place with me. It is there I would like to push in a penis and move until I make her scream with pleasure. I put my tongue at the opening and push it in as far as it will go. I take her ass in my two hands, like a big fruit, and push it upwards, and while my tongue is playing there in the mouth of her sex, my fingers press into the flesh of her ass, travel around its firmness, into its curve, and my forefinger feels the little mouth of her anus and pushes in gently.

Suddenly Mary gives a start – as if I touched off an electric spark. She moves to enclose my finger. I press it farther, all the while moving my tongue inside of her sex. She begins to moan, to undulate.

When she sinks downwards she feels my flicking finger,

when she rises upwards she meets my flicking tongue. With every move, she feels my quickening rhythm, until she has a long spasm and begins to moan like a pigeon. With my finger I feel the palpitation of pleasure, going once, twice, thrice, beating ecstatically.

She falls over, panting. 'Oh, Mandra, what have you done to me, what have you done to me!' She kisses me, drinking the salty moisture from my mouth. Her breasts fall against me as she holds me, saying again, 'Oh, Mandra, what have you done . . .'

I am invited one night to the apartment of a young society couple, the H's. It is like being on a boat because it is near the East River and the barges pass while we talk, the river is alive. Miriam is a delight to look at, a Brunhild, full-breasted, with sparkling hair, a voice that lures you to her. Her husband, Paul, is small and of the race of the imps, not a man but a faun – a lyrical animal, quick and humorous. He thinks I am beautiful. He treats me like an objet d'art. The black butler opens the door. Paul exclaims over me, my Goyaesque hood, the red flower in my hair, and hurries me into the salon to display me. Miriam is sitting cross-legged on a purple satin divan. She is a natural beauty, whereas I, an artificial one, need a setting and warmth to bloom successfully.

Their apartment is full of furnishings I find individually ugly – silver candelabra, tables with nooks for trailing flowers, enormous mulberry satin poufs, rococo objects, things full of chic, collected with snobbish playfulness, as if to say, 'We can make fun of everything created by fashion, we are above it all.'

Everything is touched with aristocratic impudence, through which I can sense the H's' fabulous life in Rome, Florence; Miriam's frequent appearances in *Vogue* wearing Chanel dresses; the pompousness of their families; their efforts to be elegantly bohemian; and their obsession with the word that is the key to society – everything must be 'amusing'.

Miriam calls me into her bedroom to show me a new bathing suit she has bought in Paris. For this, she undresses herself completely, and then takes the long piece of material and begins rolling it around herself like the primitive draping of the Balinese.

Her beauty goes to my head. She undrapes herself, walks naked around the room, and then says, 'I wish I looked like you. You are so exquisite and dainty. I am so big.'

'But that's just why I like you, Miriam.'

'Oh, your perfume, Mandra.'

She pushes her face into my shoulder under my hair and smells my skin.

I place my hand on her shoulder.

'You're the most beautiful woman I've ever seen, Miriam.'

Paul is calling out to us, 'When are you going to finish talking about clothes in there? I'm bored!'

Miriam replies, 'We're coming.' And she dresses quickly in slacks. When she comes out, Paul says, 'And now you're dressed to stay at home, and I want to take you to hear the String Man. He sings the most marvelous songs about a string and finally hangs himself on it.'

Miriam says, 'Oh, all right. I'll get dressed.' And she goes into the bathroom.

I stay behind with Paul, but soon Miriam calls me. 'Mandra, come in here and talk to me.'

I think, by this time she will be half-dressed, but no, she is standing naked in the bathroom, powdering and fixing her face.

She is as opulent as a burlesque queen. As she stands on her toes to lean towards the mirror and paint her eyelashes more carefully, I am again affected by her body. I come up behind her and watch her.

I feel a little timid. She isn't as inviting as Mary. She is, in fact, sexless, like the women at the beach or at the Turkish bath, who think nothing of their nakedness. I try a light kiss on her shoulder. She smiles at me and says, 'I wish Paul were not so irritable. I would have liked to try the bathing suit on you. I would love to see you wearing it.' She returns my kiss, on the mouth, taking care not to disturb her lipstick outline. I do not know what to do next. I want to take hold of her. I stay near her.

Then Paul comes into the bathroom without knocking and says, 'Miriam, how can you walk around like this? You mustn't mind, Mandra. It is a habit with her. She is possessed with the need to go around without clothes. Get dressed, Miriam.'

Miriam goes into her room and slips on a dress, with nothing underneath, then a fox cape, and says, 'I'm ready.'

In the car she places her hand over mine. Then she draws my hand under the fur, into a pocket of the dress, and I find myself touching her sex. We drive on in the dark.

Miriam says she wants to drive through the park first. She wants air. Paul wants to go directly to the night club, but he gives in and we drive through the park, I with my hand on Miriam's sex, fondling it and feeling my own excitement gaining so that I can hardly talk.

Miriam talks, wittily, continuously. I think to myself, 'You won't be able to go on talking in a little while.' But she does, all the time that I am caressing her in the dark, beneath the satin and the fur. I can feel her moving upwards to my touch, opening her legs a little so I can fit my entire hand between her legs. Then she grows tense under my fingers, stretching herself, and I know she is taking her pleasure. It is contagious. I feel my own orgasm without even being touched.

I am so wet that I am afraid it will show through my dress. And it must show through Miriam's dress too. We both keep our coats on as we go into the night club.

Miriam's eyes are brilliant, deep. Paul leaves us for a while and we go into the ladies' room. This time Miriam kisses my mouth fully, boldly. We arrange ourselves and return to the table.

Marianne

I shall call myself the madam of a house of literary prostitution, the madam for a group of hungry writers who were turning out erotica for sale to a 'collector'. I was the first to write, and every day I gave my work to a young woman to type up neatly.

This young woman, Marianne, was a painter, and in the evenings she typed to earn a living. She had a golden halo of hair, blue eyes, a round face, and firm and full breasts, but she tended to conceal the richness of her body rather than set it off, to disguise it under formless Bohemian clothes, loose jackets, schoolgirl skirts, raincoats. She came from a small town. She had read Proust, Krafft-Ebing, Marx, Freud.

And, of course, she had had many sexual adventures, but there is a kind of adventure in which the body does not really participate. She was deceiving herself. She thought that, having lain down with men, caressed them, and made all the prescribed gestures, she had experienced sexual life.

But it was all external. Actually her body had been numb, unformed, not yet matured. Nothing had touched her very deeply. She was still a virgin. I could feel this when she entered the room. No more than a soldier wants to admit being

43

frightened, did Marianne want to admit that she was cold, frigid. But she was being psychoanalyzed.

I could not help wondering, as I gave her my erotica to type, how it would affect her. Together with an intellectual fearlessness, curiosity, there was in her a physical prudishness which she fought hard not to betray, and it had been revealed to me accidentally by the discovery that she had never taken a sun bath naked, that the very idea of it intimidated her.

What she remembered most hauntingly was an evening with a man she had not at first responded to, and then, just as he was leaving her studio, he had pressed her hard against a wall, lifted one of her legs, and pushed into her. The strange part is that at the time she had not felt anything, but afterwards, every time she remembered this picture, she grew hot and restless. Her legs would relax, she would have given anything to feel again that big body pressing against her, pinning her to the wall, leaving her no escape, then taking her.

One day she was late in bringing me the work. I went to her studio and knocked on the door. No one answered. I pushed the door open. Marianne must have gone out on an errand.

I went to the typewriter to see how the work was going and saw a text I did not recognize. I thought perhaps I was beginning to forget what I wrote. But it could not be. That was not my writing. I began to read. And then I understood.

In the middle of her work, Marianne had been taken with the desire to write down her own experiences. This is what she wrote:

*

'There are things one reads that make you aware that you have lived nothing, felt nothing, experienced nothing up to that time. I see now that most of what happened to me was clinical, anatomical. Here were the sexes touching, mingling, but without any sparks, wildness, sensation. How can I attain this? How can I begin to *feel* – to *feel*? I want to fall in love in such a way that the mere sight of a man, even a block away from me, will shake and pierce me, will weaken me, and make me tremble and soften and melt between the legs. That is how I want to fall in love, so hard that the mere thought of him will bring on an orgasm.

'This morning while I was painting there was a very gentle knock on the door. I went to open it and there stood a rather handsome young man, but shy, embarrassed, to whom I took an instant liking.

'He slid into the studio, did not look around, kept his eyes fastened on me as if begging, and said, "A friend sent me. You are a painter; I want some work done. I wonder if you would . . . will you?"

'His speech was tangled. He blushed. He was like a woman, I thought.

'I said, "Come in and sit down," thinking that would put him at ease. Then he noticed my paintings. They were abstract. He said, "But you can draw a lifelike figure, can't you?"

' "Of course I can." I showed him my drawings.

' "They are very strong," he said, falling into a trance of admiration for one of my drawings of a muscular athlete.

' "Did you want a portrait of yourself?"

' "Why, yes – yes and no. I want a portrait. At the same time, it is a sort of unusual portrait I want, I don't know if you will . . . consent."

' "Consent to what?" I asked.

' "Well," he blurted out finally, "would you make me this kind of a portrait?" And he held up the naked athlete.

'He expected some reaction from me. I was so accustomed to men's nudity at the art school that I smiled at his shyness. I did not think there was anything odd about his demand, although it was slightly different having a naked model who paid the artist for drawing him. That was all I could see, and I told him so. Meanwhile, with the right to observe that is given to painters, I studied his violet eyes, the fine, gold, downy hair on his hands, the fine hair on the tip of his ears. He had a faunish air and a feminine evasiveness which attracted me.

'Despite his timidity, he looked healthy and rather aristo-cratic. His hands were soft and supple. He held himself well. I showed a certain professional enthusiasm which seemed to delight and encourage him.

'He said, "Do you want to start right away? I have some money with me. I can bring the rest tomorrow."

'I pointed to a corner of the room where there was a screen hiding my clothes and the washstand. But he turned his violet eyes towards me and said innocently, "Can I undress here?"

'Then I grew slightly uneasy, but I said yes. I busied myself getting drawing paper and charcoal together, moving a chair, and sharpening my charcoal. It seemed to me that he was abnormally slow in undressing, that he was waiting for my attention. I looked at him boldly, as if I were beginning my study of him, charcoal stick in hand.

'He was undressing with amazing deliberateness as if it were a choice occupation, a ritual. Once he looked at me fully in the eyes and smiled, showing his fine even teeth, and his skin was so delicate it caught the light that poured in through the big window and held it like a satin fabric.

'At this moment the charcoal in my hands felt alive, and I thought what a pleasure it would be to draw the lines of this young man, almost like caressing him. He had taken off his coat, his shirt, shoes, socks. There were only the trousers left. He held these as a stripteaser holds the folds of her dress, still looking at me. I still could not understand the gleam of pleasure that animated his face.

'Then he leaned over, unfastened his belt, and the trousers slid down. He stood completely naked before me and in a most obvious state of sexual excitement. When I saw this, there was a moment of suspense. If I protested, I would lose my fee, which I needed so badly.

'I tried to read his eyes. They seemed to say, "Do not be angry. Forgive me."

'So I tried to draw. It was a strange experience. If I drew his head, neck, arms, all was well. As soon as my eyes roved over the rest of his body I could see the effect of it on him. His sex had an almost imperceptible quiver. I was half tempted to sketch the protrusion as calmly as I had sketched his knee. But the defensive virgin in me was troubled. I thought, I must draw attentively and slowly to see if the crisis passes, or he may vent his excitement on me. But no, the young man made no move. He was transfixed and contented. I was the only one disturbed, and I did not know why.

'When I finished, he calmly dressed again, and seemed absolutely self-possessed. He walked up to me, shook my hand politely and said, "May I come tomorrow at the same time?" '

Here the manuscript ended, and Marianne entered the studio, smiling.

'Wasn't it a strange adventure?' she asked me.

'Yes, and I would like to know how you felt after he left.'

'Afterwards,' she confessed, 'it was I who was excited all day, remembering his body, and his very beautiful rigid sex. I looked at my drawings, and to one of them I added the complete image of the incident. I was actually tormented with desire. But a man like that, he is only interested in my *looking* at him.'

This might have remained a simple adventure, but to Marianne it became more important. I could see her growing obsessed with the young man. Evidently the second session had duplicated the first. Nothing was said. Marianne revealed no emotion. He did not acknowledge the condition of pleasure he was plunged in by her scrutiny of his body. Each day after that she discovered greater marvels. Every detail of his body was perfect. If only he would evince some small interest in the details of hers, but he didn't. And Marianne was growing thin and perishing with unsatisfied desire.

She was also affected by the continuous copying of other

people's adventures, for now everyone in our group who wrote gave his manuscript to her because she could be trusted. Every night little Marianne with the rich, ripe breasts bent over her typewriter and typed fervid words about violent physical happenings. Certain facts affected her more than others.

She liked violence. That is why this situation with the young man was for her the most impossible of all situations. She could not believe that he would stand in a condition of physical excitement and so clearly enjoy the mere fact of her eyes fixed on him, as if she were caressing him.

The more passive and undemonstrative he was, the more she wanted to do violence to him. She dreamed of forcing his will, but how could one force a man's will? Since she could not tempt him by her presence, how could she make him desire her?

She wished that he would fall asleep and she could have a chance to caress him, and that he would take her while he was half-conscious, half-asleep. Or she wished that he would enter the studio while she was dressing and that the sight of her body would arouse him.

Once when she expected him, she tried leaving the door ajar while she was dressing, but he looked away and took up a book.

He was impossible to arouse except by gazing on him. And Marianne was by now in a frenzy of desire for him. The drawing was coming to an end. She knew every part of his body, the color of his skin, so golden and light, every shape of his muscles and, above all, the constantly erect sex, smooth, polished, firm, tempting.

She would approach him to arrange a piece of white cardboard near him that would cast a whiter reflection or more shadows on his body. Then finally she lost control of herself and fell on her knees before the erect sex. She did not touch it, but merely looked and murmured, 'How beautiful it is!'

At this he was visibly affected. His whole sex became more rigid with pleasure. She kneeled very near it – it was almost within reach of her mouth – but again only said, 'How beautiful it is!'

Since he did not move, she came closer, her lips parted slightly, and delicately, very delicately, she touched the tip of his sex with her tongue. He did not move away. He was still watching her face and the way her tongue flicked out caressingly to touch the tip of his sex.

She licked it gently, with the delicacy of a cat, then she inserted a small portion of it in her mouth and closed her lips around it. It was quivering.

She restrained herself from doing more, for fear of encountering resistance. And when she stopped, he did not encourage her to continue. He seemed content. Marianne felt that that was all she should ask of him. She sprang to her feet and returned to her work. Inwardly she was in a turmoil. Violent images passed before her eyes. She was remembering penny movies she had seen once in Paris, of figures rolling on the grass, hands fumbling, white pants being opened by eager hands, caresses, caresses, and pleasure making the bodies curl and undulate, pleasure running over their skins like water, causing them to undulate as the wave of pleasure caught their bellies or hips, or as it ran up their spines or down their legs.

But she controlled herself with the intuitive knowledge a woman has about the tastes of the man she desires. He remained entranced, his sex erect, his body at times shivering slightly, as if pleasure coursed through it at the memory of her mouth parting to touch the smooth penis.

The day after this episode Marianne repeated her worshipful pose, her ecstasy at the beauty of his sex. Again she kneeled and prayed to this strange phallus which demanded only admiration. Again she licked it so neatly and vibrantly, sending shivers of pleasure up from the sex into his body, again she kissed it, enclosing it in her lips like some marvelous fruit, and again he trembled. Then, to her amazement, a tiny drop of a milky-white, salty substance dissolved in her mouth, the precursor of desire, and she increased her pressure and the movements of her tongue.

When she saw that he was dissolved with pleasure, she stopped, divining that perhaps if she deprived him now he might make a gesture towards fulfillment. At first he made no motion. His sex was quivering, and he was tormented with desire, then suddenly she was amazed to see his hand moving towards his sex as if he were going to satisfy himself.

Marianne grew desperate. She pushed his hand away, took his sex into her mouth again, and with her two hands she encircled his sexual parts, caressed him and absorbed him until he came.

He leaned over with gratitude, tenderness, and murmured, 'You are the first woman, the first woman, the first woman . . .'

Fred moved into the studio. But, as Marianne explained, he did not progress from the acceptance of her caresses. They lay in bed, naked, and Fred acted as if she had no sex at all. He received her tributes, frenziedly, but Marianne was left with her desire unanswered. All he would do was to place his hands between her legs. While she caressed him with her mouth his hands opened her sex like some flower and he sought for the pistil. When he felt its contractions, he willingly caressed the palpitating opening. Marianne was able to respond, but somehow this did not satisfy her hunger for his body, for his sex, and she yearned to be possessed by him more completely, to be penetrated.

It occurred to her to show him the manuscripts that she was typing. She thought this might incite him. They lay on the bed and read them together. He read the words aloud, with pleasure. He lingered over the descriptions. He read and reread, and again he took his clothes off and showed himself, but no matter what height his excitement reached he would do no more than this.

Marianne wanted him to be psychoanalyzed. She told him how much her own analysis had liberated her. He listened with interest but resisted the idea. She urged him to write, too, to write out his experiences.

At first he was shy about this, ashamed. Then, almost

surreptitiously, he began to write, hiding the pages from her when she came into the room, using a worn pencil, writing as though it were a criminal confession. It was by accident that she read what he had written. He was urgently in need of money. He had pawned his typewriter, his winter coat and his watch, and there was nothing more to be pawned.

He could not let Marianne take care of him. As it was, she tired her eyes out typing, worked late at night and never made more than was necessary for the rent and a very small supply of food. So he went to the collector to whom Marianne delivered manuscripts, and offered his own manuscript for sale, apologizing for its being written by hand. The collector, finding it difficult to read, innocently gave it to Marianne to be typed.

So Marianne found herself with her lover's manuscript in her hands. She read avidly before typing, unable to control her curiosity, in search of the secret of his passivity. This is what she read:

'Most of the time the sexual life is a secret. Everybody conspires to make it so. Even the best of friends do not tell each other the details of their sexual lives. Here with Marianne I live in a strange atmosphere. What we talk about, read about and write about is the sexual life.

'I remember an incident I had completely forgotten about. It happened when I was about fifteen and still sexually innocent. My family had taken an apartment in Paris which had many balconies, and doors giving on these balconies. In the summer I used to walk about my room naked. Once I was doing this when the doors were open, and then I noticed that a woman was watching me across the way.

'She was sitting on her balcony watching me, completely unashamed, and something drove me to pretend that I was not noticing her at all. I feared that if she knew I was aware of her she might leave.

'And being watched by her gave me the most extraordinary pleasure. I would walk about or be on my bed. She never moved. We repeated this scene every day for a week, but on the third day I had an erection.

'Could she detect this from across the street, could she see? I began to touch myself, feeling all the time how attentive she was to my every gesture. I was bathed in delicious excitement. From where I lay I could see her very luxuriant form. Looking straight at her now, I played with my sex, and finally got myself so excited that I came.

'The woman never ceased looking at me. Would she make a sign? Did it excite her to watch me? It must have. The next day I awaited her appearance with anxiety. She emerged at the same hour, sat on her balcony and looked toward me. From this distance I could not tell if she was smiling or not. I lay on my bed again.

'We did not try to meet in the street, though we were neighbors. All I remember was the pleasure I derived from this, which no other pleasure ever equaled. At the mere recollection of these episodes, I get excited. Marianne gives me somewhat the same pleasure. I like the hungry way she looks at me, admiring, worshiping me.'

When Marianne read this, she felt she would never overcome his passivity. She wept a little, feeling betrayed as a woman. Yet she loved him. He was sensitive, gentle, tender. He never hurt her feelings. He was not exactly protective, but he was fraternal, responsive to her moods. He treated her like the artist of the family, was respectful of her painting, carried her canvases, wanted to be useful to her.

She was a monitor in a painting class. He loved to accompany her there in the morning with the pretext of carrying her paints. But soon she saw that he had another purpose. He was passionately interested in the models. Not in them personally, but in their experience of posing. He wanted to be a model.

At this Marianne rebelled. If he had not derived a sexual pleasure from being looked at, she might not have minded. But knowing this, it was as if he were giving himself to the whole class. She could not bear the thought. She fought him.

But he was possessed by the idea and finally was accepted as a model. That day Marianne refused to go to the class. She stayed at home and wept like a jealous woman who knows her lover is with another woman.

She raged. She tore up her drawings of him as if to tear his image from her eyes, the image of his golden, smooth, perfect body. Even if the students were indifferent to the models, he was reacting to their eyes, and Marianne could not bear it.

This incident began to separate them. It seemed as if the more pleasure she gave him, the more he succumbed to his vice, and sought it unceasingly.

Soon they were completely estranged. And Marianne was left alone again to type out erotica.